CHEER UP LITTLE NODDY!

BY

Enid Blyton

CONTENTS

LONDON
SAMPSON LOW, MARSTON & CO., LTD.
AND RICHARDS PRESS LTD.

NODDY RODE ON THE DONKEY'S BACK AND WAVED
PROUDLY TO EVERYONE HE MET.

6

1. TWO BAD LITTLE BEARS

NODDY was washing his little car one morning, singing very loudly, because he felt so happy. He splashed water about, and the car jiggled and hooted because it felt happy too.

Noddy sang and sang, and rubbed and polished, his head nodding all the time. It was nice to listen to him.

> "The sun is shining
> And so is my car,
> It's a beautiful morning,
> How happy we are!
> Parp-parp-parp!

Soon we'll be speeding
Away down the street,
Hooting and waving
To friends that we meet,
Parp-parp-parp!

And now I have finished,
So in I will jump,
And drive away quickly,
A-bumpety-bump,
Parp-parp-parp!"

The little car joined in at the "parp-parps",
and jiggled happily. Just as Noddy was giving it
the very last rub, someone called to him.

"Hallo, Noddy! Can we help you?"

Noddy looked round and saw little Tubby Bear
leaning on the wall, with another little bear beside
him.

"Well, I've just finished," said Noddy. "Who's
that bear with you?"

"My cousin, Tommy Bear," said Tubby. "He's

come to spend the day with me. Do you think he could just *sit* in your car for a minute? He does so love cars."

"I can drive," said Tommy Bear, proudly.

"Well, you needn't think I'll let you drive *my* car," said Noddy. "You can just *sit* in it, and nothing else. Tubby, sit with him, and don't let him do anything silly. I'm going to wash my hands, and take off my overall—then I'm going out to look for passengers."

He went into his little house, whistling. Tubby Bear and Tommy Bear jumped over the wall in delight, and ran to where the little car stood outside Noddy's garage in the sunshine. Tommy Bear climbed into the driver's seat, and pressed the hooter. "PARP-PARP-PARP-PARP-PARP!"

9

"Stop that noise!" yelled Noddy, putting his head out of the window. "Get out, Tommy Bear. Stop hooting. GET OUT, I SAY!"

But Tommy was *not* going to get out. He was enjoying himself. How lovely to sit in such a dear little car, and hoot as if it belonged to him!

Then a very naughty thought came into his head. If only he could drive it just a *little* way! Just down the road and back. He whispered into Tubby's ear, and Tubby nodded at once. "I'll have a turn too," he said.

And, to the little car's enormous surprise, Tommy Bear guided it out into the road! The car was very cross. It didn't like to be driven by anyone but Noddy. It began to hoot loudly, trying to tell Noddy what was happening, and Noddy put his head out of the window once more, ready to shout at the two little bears again.

He could not believe

TO THE LITTLE CAR'S ENORMOUS SURPRISE, TOMMY
BEAR GUIDED IT OUT INTO THE ROAD!

his eyes when he saw his car going down the road—slowly at first, then faster, and then very fast indeed!

"Stop, little car, stop! Come back!" he shouted, running out of his front gate. He was just in time to see the car turn a corner at top speed, hooting madly. Noddy ran out into the road, feeling

quite shocked. "Tommy Bear will have an accident! I know he will!" said poor Noddy, nodding his head up and down very fast indeed.

The two little bears were enjoying themselves. They raced into the High Street, where everyone was busy shopping, the little car still hooting angrily. Mr. Plod the policeman was standing in the middle of the road, directing the traffic, and he was most astonished to see Noddy's car racing along at top speed, coming straight at him.

"What do you think you are doing, Noddy?" he yelled, and jumped aside just in time, falling over, bump! He stared after the little car in surprise. "It *wasn't* Noddy driving!" he said. "Who was it then? Wait till I get hold of him! There will be a very hard spanking for SOMEBODY!"

Poor Noddy was still standing in the road, wondering what to do. "No good going after my car," he said to himself. "I don't even know where it is. How DARE that nasty little Tommy Bear drive it away? And to think Tubby Bear let him! I'll smack them! I'll pull their noses! I'll tread on their toes! I'll—well, no, I'd better not. I'll go and tell Mr. Plod, he'll know what to do!"

So he set off to find Mr.
Plod—but on the way
whom should he meet
but Big-Ears, riding his
bicycle at top speed,
ringing his bell madly.
"Ting-a-ling-a-
ting-a-ling-a-ling-
a-ting!"

"Big-Ears! BIG-EARS! Stop! I've news for
you!" shouted Noddy. Big-Ears put on his brakes
and stopped so suddenly that he nearly flew over
his handle-bars.

"Noddy! I was looking for you!" he cried.
"Noddy, there's been an accident. Oh, Noddy,
your poor little car! Those two bad little bears
ran it into a tree near my Toadstool House,
and . . ."

"Big-Ears—where is it? Is it badly hurt?" cried
Noddy, and big tears ran down his cheeks.
"Oh, I was afraid of that! What about the little
bears?"

"Not even scratched or bruised!" said Big-
Ears. "They jumped out and ran away—but wait
till I see them again. . . . I'll—I'll—well, I really
don't know *what* I'll do!"

14

2. EVERYONE IS KIND TO NODDY

BIG-EARS and Noddy went off to kind Mr.
Golly, who owned the garage in Toyland
Village. He was very upset to hear about Noddy's
car. "I'll send the breakdown van up to Big-
Ears' house and collect it," he said. "Now don't
you worry—I'll soon have it mended for you!"

Oh dear, oh dear—when Noddy saw his poor
little car he was very sad indeed. The front
was smashed in, and the lamps were broken, and
one wheel was almost off. Noddy cried when he
saw it, but Mr. Golly comforted him, and so did
Big-Ears.

"It can be mended!" said Mr. Golly. "I'll make it as good as new."

"It can't even say 'Parp-parp' to me," wept Noddy.

"Parp-parp," said the car suddenly, in a small hoarse voice, and Noddy went to stroke it and pat it, just as if it were a dog. "Don't worry!" he said to his little car. "I'll see that you are mended, even if it costs me all the money I earn in a year. I'll drive you again, little car, so don't be sad—and you will soon sleep in your own little garage again!"

"Parp-parp!" said the car once more, sounding happier, and was soon lifted on to kind Mr.

Golly's breakdown van, and taken away through Toadstool Wood. Noddy stayed behind with Big-Ears, who made some hot cocoa, and set out big slices of fruit cake on his little table. Whiskers the cat came and sat on Noddy's knee, purring loudly, rubbing his big soft head against him. Noddy listened to him.

"He's telling me to eat some fruit cake and feel better," he told Big-Ears. "So I think I will. Big-Ears, what shall I do to earn money now that my car is broken?"

"Well now, let's think," said Big-Ears, helping himself to fruit cake, too. "You could borrow a barrow, and do people's shopping for them, bringing everything back in the barrow."

"Oh *yes*—and I could charge sixpence a time," said Noddy, drinking his cocoa.

"And you could go to the market and buy flowers and fruit cheaply, and sell them to anyone in Toyland Village who wants them," said Big-Ears. "You could charge an extra penny on everything you sell, to pay for your trouble."

"Dear me—you do have some good ideas, Big-Ears," said Noddy, pleased. "I'll barrow a borrow tomorrow—I mean, I'll morrow a borrow tomarrow—no, no— I'll borrow a marrow tomorrow—oh, Big-Ears, aren't I silly! I can't say it right!"

Big-Ears laughed, and Noddy began to laugh too. "*That's* better!" said Big-Ears. "Laughing is better than crying any day. Well—borrow a marrow, or morrow a barrow—whichever you like—so long as you can wheel goods in it and earn money! Have another slice of cake?"

Noddy felt much better when he left Big-Ears and Whiskers, and went off down to Toyland Village again. Everyone he met came up to tell him how sorry they were about his car, and they all promised to give him errands to do if he could borrow a barrow.

BIG-EARS LAUGHED, AND NODDY BEGAN
TO LAUGH TOO.

19

"Mr. Tubby Bear will lend you his," said Miss Fluffy-Cat. "He and Mrs. Tubby Bear are so very sorry about your car, Noddy. Tubby Bear has had a good spanking already, and it serves him right—and Tommy Bear has disappeared. He's afraid to go back to the Tubby Bears', and he hasn't gone home, either. Nobody knows where he is, the little nuisance."

"Just let me catch him!" said Noddy, fiercely. "I'll pull his hair, I'll tread on his toes, I'll take away his grunt, I'll . . ."

"That won't bring your car back, Noddy," said Miss Fluffy-Cat. "I expect he's very sorry now and is afraid to show his furry face."

Noddy went to Mr. Tubby to ask if he could borrow his barrow. "Of course!" said Mr. Tubby, putting his big arm round Noddy. "We'll help you all we can, Noddy. We've spanked Tubby Bear—though it was Tommy Bear who drove off your car—and we'll help to pay the garage bill for mending it. But I'm afraid it will be a very *big* bill. Tubby wants to give you the money out of his money box—and Mrs. Tubby Bear says she'll do all your washing for you and your mending too, to show you how sorry *she* is."

It wasn't only the Tubby Bears who were kind. Little Tessie Bear came hurrying to see Noddy when she heard the news. She hugged him tightly, and the Bumpy-Dog, who had come with her, licked Noddy so much that he had to get a towel to wipe his face.

"Bumpy, don't!" he said. "I know you lick me because you like me, but your tongue's so *wet*!

I shall have to keep a towel in my pocket instead of a hanky if you go on like this. Oooh—DON'T jump up at me like that! You'll knock me over!"

"BUMPY! Go outside," said Tessie Bear, and Bumpy put down his tail and trotted out, looking very much upset. "He wants to help you too," said Tessie. "But he's so *very* excitable. Dear Noddy—I'll help all I can. I'll take one handle of Mr. Tubby's barrow, and help you to wheel it."

"Oh no, Tessie—I couldn't let you do that," said Noddy. "I'm very strong. Feel my arms! Hard as anything, aren't they?"

"Yes. You're very, very strong," said Tessie, feeling his arms. "Noddy, I've brought you some toffee. I made it myself for you."

People really were very kind to Noddy. Miss Fluffy-Cat sent him a meat-pie she had baked. Sally Skittle sent her little skittle children along with some lovely jam-tarts. It was a

pity that the Bumpy-Dog was at the gate when the Skittle family came with the tarts, because he thought they were for him, and he had eaten seven by the time Noddy came out with a big dish!

Even the old Wobbly-Man wobbled along with a box of chocolates. The Bumpy-Dog leapt up at him in delight when he met him outside Noddy's house, and the Wobbly-Man wobbled to and fro so much that he dropped all the chocolates. Wasn't the Bumpy-Dog pleased!

But Noddy wasn't. He chased Bumpy away with a stick, and Bumpy fled in horror. A stick! Oh no, he wasn't going to stop with Noddy *and* a stick! He went back to Tessie Bear's and put himself to bed in his kennel, wishing he had had time to lick up a few more of the spilt chocolates.

3. NODDY IS VERY, VERY BUSY

NEXT day Noddy was very, very busy. He took Mr. Tubby's barrow and went to ask for jobs. He sang a little song as he went.

"Parcels fetched
And shopping done,
Letters posted,
Errands run!

Windows cleaned
And doorsteps too,
Goods delivered,
All day through!

If you're wanting
Cakes for tea,
Or eggs for supper,
Shout for ME!"

Well, so many people wanted to help Noddy that he soon had more jobs than he could do! Tessie Bear met him in the village, wheeling Mr. Tubby Bear's big barrow. It was quite full of shopping that he had fetched for a great many people. Noddy pushed the barrow along, looking very hot.

"Noddy! Come and have an ice-cream," said Tessie. "You look hot."

"Well, I *am* hot!" said Noddy. "But I'm earning

a lot of money, Tessie. I think I'll very soon be able to pay for my car being mended. I don't think I'll stop for an ice-cream, thank you. I promised Mrs. Skittle I'd take all her shopping home in time for the Skittle children's dinner."

Off he went, wheeling the heavy barrow. Tessie Bear stared after him. "Oh dear—he'll tire himself out," she thought. "He's so little, and the barrow is so BIG!"

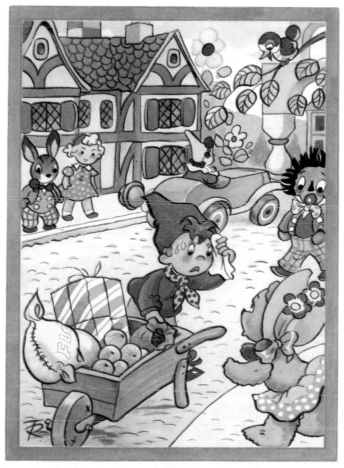

"NODDY! COME AND HAVE AN ICE-CREAM,"
SAID TESSIE.

Noddy really did work hard that first day. The second day was worse, because Mr. Noah sent Katie Kangaroo to him, to ask if he could please fetch all the food for the Noah's Ark animals that day.

"Good gracious!" said Noddy. "It won't all go into my barrow, Katie Kangaroo, even if I pile it up high."

"Well, you could fill the barrow a second time, couldn't you?" said Katie. "I'll come along with you and put some things into my pouch."

But even though she did that, there were three barrow-loads of food to take to the Ark. Noddy began to feel as if his arms would fall off. Mrs. Noah was sorry for him. "Can't you get a little

hand-cart?" she said. "That would be easier for you than pushing a heavy barrow."

28

So Noddy borrowed a little hand-cart from Tessie's Uncle Bear the next day, and found it easier, because he could pull it by the handle instead of having to *push* it like a barrow.

How he panted and puffed! He pulled the little four-wheeled cart about all day long, fetching shopping and posting parcels, and collecting washing for such a lot of people.

Big-Ears gave him a job too. "Will you collect a box for me at the railway station?" he said. "It will have a new tea-set in it, so be careful, Noddy. I'll pay you a whole shilling if you bring it up to my house without one single thing broken." So Noddy collected the big box from the porter

at the railway station just after the train had gone. Goodness—what a big one! And how heavy! It took both Noddy *and* the porter to carry it to the little handcart.

"My word—I hope you haven't very far to take this heavy box," said the porter.

"Well, I *have*!" said Noddy. "It's for Big-Ears, my friend, and he lives right in the middle of Toadstool Wood. I *shall* want to sit down when I get there—I'll sit for an hour, I should think, in his comfy armchair."

Poor little Noddy! He panted and puffed up the path through the wood to Big-Ears' house, and all the little rabbits came out to watch him. Two tried to help him with the cart, and he hadn't even enough breath left to say thank you!

He took it to Big-Ears' front door and knocked. Then he sat down on the path, panting.

Big-Ears opened the door. "Oh, you good little Noddy!" he said, pleased. "You've brought my new tea-set safely. Help me in with it."

"I can't," said Noddy, in a very small voice. "I can't get up. My legs won't let me. They're so tired."

"Noddy! You poor little fellow!" cried Big-Ears, and ran to help him. "Come along—

lean on me. I've a fine tea waiting for you."

"I don't want any," said Noddy. "I'm too tired to eat. My teeth won't bite, and my throat won't swallow."

"Dear me—how silly we've all been, giving you so many jobs to do, thinking we were helping you!" said Big-Ears, settling Noddy into his best armchair. "There now—lie back, and shut your eyes. I'll make the tea and butter the scones."

"I can't eat any scones," said Noddy, still speaking in a very small voice, and at once fell asleep. Big-Ears stood and looked at him.

"Poor little Noddy! Working so hard! And after all, it wasn't *his* fault that his car has to be mended. Tubby Bear and Tommy Bear ought to be doing all this work, not Noddy. But goodness knows where Tommy has got to—and as for that lazy little Tubby, he'd sit down and rest half the time!" Big-Ears frowned, and then looked out of the window at the four-wheeled hand-cart with the big box inside.

"Noddy can't pull that about all day long. It's too heavy. I wonder if I could get a horse to pull it for him. A *nice* little horse. No—I don't know anyone with a horse to lend. What a pity!" Big-Ears let Noddy sleep. He carried the box from the hand-cart into his house and began to unpack the tea-set. Not one single thing was broken. Noddy still slept on and on, cuddled down in the armchair.

Then away in the distance Big-Ears heard a loud voice calling. Who ever was this coming along? He listened hard, and heard a song he knew very well.

"I'm the Saucepan Man, the Saucepan Man,
   I can sell you a kettle or a pan,
   Or a nice little watering can,
   Because I am the Saucepan Man."

"Saucepans for SALE!
   Saucepans for SALE!"

32

4. THE OLD SAUCEPAN MAN

"THAT'S the old Saucepan Man," said Big-Ears, pleased. "He must have known I wanted a new saucepan and a kettle as well. And his dear little donkey, Ee-Aw, is with him too. Good!"

He went to the door and shouted. "Hey, Saucepan Man. Come and have some tea!"

The Saucepan Man came up, beaming all over his jolly face. He was hung about with saucepans and kettles and pans, which made a tremendous jingling, clattering noise. The noise had made him quite deaf, so he was very, very hard of hearing.

With him, trotting behind, was his dear little donkey, Ee-Aw, hung about with saucepans and kettles, too. What a noise they made—clitter, clatter, jingle, jangle—and clippity-clop went

Ee-Aw's hooves as he came up the path.

"Hallo, Saucepan," said Big-Ears. "Come in. Tea's just ready. I've Noddy here too, but he's asleep."

Soon he and Saucepan were eating hot scones, and Saucepan was telling Big-Ears all about his adventures. "I wish Noddy would wake up and hear them too," he said. "Oh look at Ee-Aw peeping in at the window. May I give him a hot scone?"

Saucepan was so deaf that when Big-Ears spoke to him he had to shout at the top of his voice—but not even the shouting awoke Noddy. He slept on and on and on.

"Big-Ears, I've come to ask you something," said Saucepan, eating his fifth scone. "I want your help. I'm going to visit my old aunt Katie Kettle—you may have heard of her. She lives over the sea."

"Good gracious! Are you going off in a boat then?" said Big-Ears. "Whatever will Ee-Aw the donkey say to that?"

"Well, he just won't *come*," said Saucepan. "I've talked and talked to him about it, but he shakes his head every time and stamps his hoof. You just see!" He turned to where Ee-Aw was still staring in at the window and called to him. "Ee-Aw—you *will* come in a boat with me across the sea, won't you?"

Ee-Aw at once shook his head firmly from side to side, and stamped his hoof. "There you are," said Saucepan. "He just *won't* come. He must be frightened of crabs or something. Anyway, I've come to ask you if you'll please keep him for me while I am gone."

"Keep your *donkey*!" said Big-Ears. "Of course not. Don't be silly. I've nowhere to keep a *donkey*. You can't go about asking people to keep donkeys, you know."

"Well, I kept Whiskers, your cat, for you, and looked after him once, when *you* went away," said Saucepan.

"That's different," said Big-Ears. "A donkey is *much* bigger than a cat, Saucepan. Perhaps you haven't noticed that?"

"Oh well—I'll go and ask someone else to have Ee-Aw," said Saucepan, in a huff, and got up with a great clatter and jingle. "He's quite useful. He'll give people rides, or carry sacks of potatoes and things like that. Goodbye, Big-Ears. I'll try and catch a whale for you when I'm on the sea. Or would that be too big for you to cook for your dinner? Goodbye!"

Just as Saucepan was walking out of the door looking very cross, a Grand Idea came to Big-Ears and he yelled loudly after the Saucepan Man.

"SAUCEPAN! SAUCEPAN! I'VE A WONDERFUL IDEA!"
YELLED BIG-EARS.

37

"Saucepan! SAUCEPAN! I've a wonderful idea! Come back! I'll keep your donkey for you —or at least my friend Noddy here will keep him —and use him too! SAUCEPAN, stop being cross and COME BACK!"

Saucepan came back, looking surprised. "Did I hear you shouting at me?" he said. "What do you want?"

Big-Ears told him all over again, and Saucepan looked pleased. "All right. I'll leave Ee-Aw with you," he said. "He'll be quite good. He likes you. I really must go, Big-Ears, or I shall miss my train."

"Train? But I thought you were going over the sea!" said Big-Ears, astonished.

"Dear me, yes—so I am," said Saucepan. "Good thing you reminded me. I've a boat to catch, of course, not a train. Goodbye, Big-Ears. Be kind to Ee-Aw. I'll soon be back."

5. NODDY AND THE DONKEY

BIG-EARS went out to see the Saucepan Man off. While he was at the front gate, waving to him, Noddy woke up. He was MOST surprised to see a donkey's face looking in at the window.

"What a nice little donkey!" he thought. "Looking in at the window too! I must still be asleep and dreaming. Hallo, little donkey!"

"Ee-aw, ee-aw," said the donkey, waving his long, furry ears about. Big-Ears came back just then, and Noddy called out to him.

"Oh—*you're* in my dream too, Big-Ears, as well as the donkey. Isn't he sweet! I wish he was mine!"

"You *aren't* dreaming," said Big-Ears. "That's a *real* donkey, Noddy. It belongs to old Saucepan. And do you know what? You can borrow him to carry all your goods and shopping and parcels!"

"*Borrow* him! Borrow a *donkey*!" said Noddy, in great astonishment. "This is certainly a dream I'm having. Nobody's ever offered to lend me a donkey before. I *wish* I was awake. I really *would* find a donkey a help in carrying all the packages and parcels. My arms are so very tired."

"You poor little fellow!" said Big-Ears. "What have we all been thinking of, to let you work so hard! It's true about the donkey, Noddy. Sauce-pan has gone to visit his Aunt Kettle over the sea, and he's left his donkey with me, and I thought he could carry all your things for you."

"Oh, I'm so happy!" said Noddy, running to Big-Ears. "To think I won't have to push a barrow or pull a cart any more! Thank you, Big-Ears, thank you! Oh, I must go and talk to the donkey. What's his name? Can I bring him indoors?"

"No, certainly not," said Big-Ears. "There wouldn't be much left of my little house if Ee-Aw gallivanted round it!"

"Oh, does he gallivant?" said Noddy. "What's

gallivanting? Can *I* gallivant? I'll gallivant out to speak to Ee-Aw! Watch me gallivant, Big-Ears! Oh, I'm so happy again!"

Ee-Aw was delighted to see little Noddy, and butted him gently with his nose. Noddy flung his arms round the donkey's neck and hugged him.

"Ee-aw!" said the donkey, in delight, and suddenly did a little dance, clip-clopping all over the place. Big-Ears laughed. Well, well—now everything would be fine! Noddy would have someone to carry his things, and pull his little cart—and Ee-Aw would be happy while the Saucepan Man was away.

"Big-Ears, I could eat some tea now," said Noddy. "I suddenly don't feel tired any more. And after tea Ee-Aw and I are going to gallivant down to Toyland Village, and fetch some things for Mr. Noah. Ee-Aw says he knows how to gallivant. He nodded his head when I asked him. Big-Ears, isn't he a DEAR little donkey?"

Well, Noddy had a wonderful time now that he had a donkey to help him. He trotted him down to Toyland Village, dragging the little hand-cart behind him, and how everyone stared to see Noddy riding on a donkey!

He sang a merry song as they trotted down the street.

"Oh, I've a little donkey
 That gallivants along,
 I know he's rather little,
 But he's very, VERY strong!
 He can trot and canter,
 He can say 'Ee-aw!'
 He's just the nicest donkey
 I ever, ever saw!
 EE-AW! EE-AW!

42

His tail is very frisky,
His ears are very long,
And all the time he's
   trotting
He sings his 'ee-aw' song.
Just see us both together,
Trotting quick and gay,
Galli-gallivanting,
Happy all the day!
EE-AW! EE-AW!"

Every time Noddy came to the Ee-aw part, the little donkey joined in. The Skittle children ran after him, delighted, and the Wobbly-Man wobbled as fast as he could to keep up with him. As for Mr. Plod he couldn't believe his eyes when he suddenly saw Noddy trotting by at top speed on a *donkey*.

"Hey—what do you think you're doing on that donkey?" shouted Mr. Plod.

"I'm gallivanting!" shouted Noddy. "We're *both* gallivanting! You come and gallivant too, Mr. Plod!"

Noddy had a marvellous time with Ee-Aw that evening. Everyone came to pat the little donkey, and promised Noddy to bring him plenty of goods to deliver the next day.

"You can put your parcels and sacks in this little cart that Ee-Aw is dragging behind him," said Noddy. "I'll ride on his back, and it won't take us any time to take the goods here and there. Isn't he a darling?"

"Yes. Yes he *is*," said everyone, patting him. Tessie Bear rushed into the greengrocer's shop and bought him a carrot. Ee-Aw was so surprised. He ate the carrot, and then tried to eat the flowers round Tessie's hat.

"No, Ee-Aw, no," said Noddy. "Tessie, do take off your hat before he eats it as well as the flowers! We'd better go, I think. He's getting a bit frisky —what Big-Ears would call *gallivanty*. Come on, Ee-Aw, gallivant away. That's right—clip-clop-clippetty-clop—ooh, mind that monkey, you nearly trod on his tail."

44

"COME ON, EE-AW, GALLIVANT AWAY," CRIED NODDY.
"OH, MIND THAT MONKEY!"

Noddy came to his little House-For-One and slid down off Ee-Aw's furry back. Ee-Aw liked the look of the house very much, and at once trotted up the path to the door.

"Ee-Aw, I really think you'd better go into the garage," said Noddy. "My dear little car has had an accident, so it's empty. I don't think you'd behave very well inside a house."

But Ee-Aw had other ideas. He wanted to see Noddy's house, and as soon as Noddy opened the door, in he trotted. He brayed in delight.

"Ee-aw, Ee-aw, nicest house I ever saw!" he seemed to say, and sat down on one of Noddy's chairs. But he was much too heavy, and the chair creaked and broke. Ee-Aw was dreadfully upset, and ran straight out of the house braying mournfully.

Noddy ran after him, shouting, "It's all right, Ee-Aw, I forgive you! PLEASE don't run away! Ee-Aw, I'll give you carrots for your supper. EE-AW, COME BACK."

Then the little donkey trotted back, hanging his head in shame. He went straight into the garage this time, and lay down on the floor.

"I'll bring you some straw to lie on, for a nice bed," said Noddy. "And I'll leave the door open so that you won't be in the dark. But don't gallivant away, will you? Oh, I *do* like that word. Gallivant, gallivant, gallivant away, I'd *like* to go a-gallivanting, every single day! That's a new little song I've made up for *you*, Ee-Aw."

Soon Noddy had brought some straw for Ee-Aw, and pulled some new carrots from his garden. Mrs. Tubby Bear was most astonished to see the donkey in the garage. She was still feeling very very sorry because Tubby and Tommy Bear had had an accident with Noddy's car, and she had brought Noddy a lovely iced cake.

"Ee-aw!" said the donkey, joyfully, thinking

it was for him. Noddy just saved the cake in time!

"No—this is for *me*!" he said. "The *carrots* are for you! Oh, Ee-Aw—what fun we'll have tomorrow when we go round delivering our goods and parcels together!"

6. STOP IT, BUMPY-DOG!

NODDY awoke very early the next morning, hearing a most peculiar noise nearby. He sat up in bed and listened. "Cloppetty-clippetty-cloppetty-clip, cloppetty. . . ."

"Goodness—it's Ee-Aw doing a little gallivant round my garage!" said Noddy. "He'll wake up everyone!"

So he went out to the garage and opened the door. Ee-Aw was so pleased to see Noddy that he ran straight at him, and knocked him over.

"You're as bad as the Bumpy-Dog!" said Noddy. "Ee-Aw, stop racing round the garage. You're making a terrible noise, and it's not even six o'clock yet."

"Ee-aw, ee-aw!" said the donkey, rubbing his nose lovingly against Noddy's shoulder. Then he snuffled gently into Noddy's ear. Noddy

49

couldn't help feeling very loving too—really, Ee-Aw was such a *dear* little donkey!

"Come into my house—but be very quiet, because I want to go to sleep again," said Noddy. "We've a hard day's work to do, you know." He led Ee-Aw into his house, and the donkey at once lay down on the floor, afraid of trying to sit on a chair again. Noddy climbed into bed.

Ee-Aw put his head on the pillow to be as near Noddy as he could, and he went to sleep too. When the milkman came, and looked in at the window, he was *most* astonished. Whatever next!

Noddy and the donkey had a very exciting time that day! Everyone came hurrying up with goods to be taken here and there, with lists of shopping for Noddy to do, and orders for him to go to the market and buy fruit and vegetables for them.

WUFF! WUFF!

Noddy felt very important indeed. He set off with Ee-Aw, the little hand-cart trundling along behind them. Soon it was full of parcels and sacks. Noddy rode on the donkey's back, and waved proudly to everyone he met.

And then the Bumpy-Dog came running by and suddenly saw Noddy high up on the donkey's back. He simply couldn't believe it! He hadn't heard anything about Ee-Aw and was most excited to see Noddy riding him.

He raced up, barking madly. "Wuff-WUFF-WUFFY-WUFF!" Ee-Aw had a terrible fright when he heard Bumpy, and felt his nose against his hooves. He at once began to gallop at top speed, with the Bumpy-Dog after him.

The little cart bumped along, jolting here and there, and one by one all the parcels and sacks shot out into the road. Noddy was very angry indeed. He pulled at the donkey's ears, and yelled at Bumpy-Dog.

"Stop it, Bumpy-Dog! Have you gone mad? Bumpy, GO AWAY! Ee-Aw, slow down! Stop *galloping*, Ee-Aw! Oh my goodness, they're both crazy now, mad as can be! Oh, my parcels and sacks! Bumpy, GO AWAY! My goodness, now there's Mr. Plod. Ee-Aw, stop! STOP!"

But Ee-Aw didn't stop, and Mr. Plod suddenly found himself sitting down hard in the road, while a mad donkey, a mad dog and a mad hand-cart raced by him at sixty miles an hour. Mr. Plod was very, very angry. He stared after the cloud of dust in the distance.

"Was that NODDY on the donkey's back?

What in the world does he think he's doing? I'll put him in prison! As for that Bumpy-Dog, he ought to live inside a kennel without any door! Where's my helmet?"

"Please, Mr. Plod, you're sitting on it," said Katie Kitten, with a sudden giggle. "Mr. Plod, shall I pick up all the things that have fallen out of Noddy's cart?"

Well, Katie Kitten, Gilbert Golly, Miss Fluffy-Cat and Sally Skittle all helped to pick up the things that had fallen out of Noddy's cart. Then they waited for Noddy and Ee-Aw to come back.

"There they are," said Katie. "Goodness, doesn't Noddy look cross!"

He certainly did. He was cross with Ee-Aw and cross with Bumpy and cross with everybody.

"What's the good of me trying to help everyone?" he shouted. "My donkey ran away, Bumpy-Dog went mad, and my little cart's gone, and all my parcels! Mr. Plod, arrest the Bumpy-Dog and put him in prison."

Mr. Plod had never seen Noddy so angry before. "Now, now!" he said. "Calm yourself, Noddy. I can see it wasn't your fault that I was knocked down. All your goods are safe. But where is your cart?"

"Goodness knows!" said Noddy. "But I'm not going to use it again while I have Ee-Aw! Galloping away like that with a cart full of things! He'll have to carry them on his back in future and I shall walk beside him, holding his bridle firmly. What with a gallivanting donkey, and

a gallivanting dog, I'm—I'm—well, I feel as if *I* want to gallivant too, and knock everyone down!"

Tessie Bear came up then, and laughed. She slipped her little paw into Noddy's hand. "Don't worry, Noddy! And don't be cross any more.

We'll all help to put the things on Ee-Aw's back.
Look—he's sorry he galloped away. He won't do
it again."

"Where's that Bumpy-Dog?" said Noddy, still
looking fierce. "I'll give him such a spanking!
Behaving like that, and upsetting everything!"

Bumpy was hiding behind the donkey. When
he heard Noddy's angry voice he crept out and
went to him. He suddenly sat up on his hind legs
and begged, looking at Noddy out of big, sad
eyes. A large tear rolled all the way down his
nose and dripped on to the ground. Plop!

"He's begging you to forgive him," said Tessie.

"All right," said Noddy. "I forgive you,
Bumpy." Bumpy was so overjoyed that he suddenly leapt at Noddy, licking him everywhere—
and down went poor Noddy. BUMP!

"Get OFF me, Bumpy!" he groaned.
"What a dog! Stop licking me.
Tessie, pull him off. I
really *must* get on with
my work."

7. HURRAY! HURRAY!

NODDY and Ee-Aw worked very hard for three whole days after that. Noddy piled everything on to Ee-Aw's back, and either rode him or walked beside him. Ee-Aw slept in Noddy's garage every night, and was really very good except that he sometimes took it into his head to gallop at top speed, and poor Noddy had to run till he was quite out of breath.

"Still, you are very useful, Ee-Aw," he said. "I think I've enough money now to pay for my car being mended. Oh, I WISH my little car was back. I do miss it so. I went to look at it yesterday, Ee-Aw, and it looked dreadful—its wheels were off, and its hooter was gone, and—and—

no, I mustn't think about it, else I'll howl just like Bumpy does when *he's* upset."

HURRAY! HURRAY!

The next day Noddy had a shock! The Saucepan Man arrived very suddenly, clanking and clinking as usual! "Where's Ee-Aw?" he said. "I want him. I've missed him so much. I've come to take him back."

"But, SAUCEPAN! You lent him to me till my little car was mended!" said Noddy. "Didn't you go to see your Aunt Kettle?"

"No. I was seasick on the boat, and turned back," said Saucepan. "Where's Ee-Aw?"

"There he is—with little Tessie Bear," said Noddy, pointing. "She always gives him a carrot each morning. EE-AW! EE-AW! LOOK WHO'S HERE!"

Well, Ee-Aw nearly went mad with delight when he saw the old Saucepan Man. He galloped up at top speed and almost knocked him over, ee-awing so loudly that everyone looked out of their windows to see what the noise could be. Saucepan put his arms round Ee-Aw's neck, and they went off up the street together, without even saying goodbye to little

Noddy! They *were* so pleased to have one another again!

Noddy felt left-out and lonely. *Now* what was he to do? He couldn't pull that heavy hand-cart again, or wheel that big barrow. He sat down on the kerb, feeling sad. "Ee-Aw *might* have said goodbye to me," he thought. "Oh dear—how miserable I feel without my dear little car!"

Look, Noddy—look what's coming down the street, all by itself, looking for you! It's been to your little House-For-One, and you weren't there. It looked into the garage but that was empty. It ran up to Big-Ears' house, and there was no one there either. Noddy, lift your head, and see what's coming down the street!

But Noddy didn't lift his head. He sat on the kerb, very lonely indeed. Then he felt something nudge him, and he heard a soft little sound in his ear. "Parp-parp!"

Ah—*then* he looked up! A big smile came over his face, and he leapt to his feet. "My little car! You're mended! You've come to find me!

You look BEAUTIFUL, BEAUTIFUL, BEAUTI-
FUL! Oh, I'm *so* happy!"

"Parp-parp," said the little car, and jiggled about
all round Noddy. Then it butted him gently, and
opened one of its doors all by itself.

"Yes, yes—I'm going to get in and drive you!"
said Noddy, joyfully. "Let me just look at you a
minute—you look so fine, so clean, so shiny! Oh,
I've missed you so! Have you missed *me*, little
car?"

"PARP-PARP-PARP!" said the car very loudly
indeed, and jiggled about again. Noddy jumped
into the driving seat, and drove away down the
street, singing loudly and joyfully. The little
car hooted, and everyone came running to doors
and windows to see what was happening.

"It's Noddy! He's got his car back! It's
mended. Hurrah, Noddy, hurrah!"

CHEER UP, LITTLE NODDY!

Noddy drove all round Toyland Village singing loudly. It was such a happy song. Listen!

"My car is mended, it's good as new,
  Parp-parp!
  If you want a ride, it's ready for you,
  Parp-parp!
  We'll take you wherever you want to go,
  We'll drive you fast and we'll drive you slow,
  PARP-PARP-PARP!
  So hurry along and jump inside,
  Hurray!
  You'll have a perfectly lovely ride,
  Hurray!
  Oh, we're so happy, my car and I,
  We can't HELP singing as we go by,
  HURRAY! HURRAY!"

LOOK FOR
THE NEXT
NODDY
BOOK